# Boats
## Byron Barton

**HarperCollins**Publishers

Library of Congress Cataloging-in-Publication Data   Barton, Byron. Boats. Summary: Depicts
several kinds of boats and ships.   1.  Boats and boating—Juvenile literature.   2.  Ships—Juvenile
literature.   [1.  Boats and boating.   2.  Ships.]  I. Title.  VM150.B36  1986     387.2  [E]  85-47900
ISBN 0-694-00059-0.—0-690-04536-0 (lib. bdg.)

# On the water

**there goes a rowboat.**

**Here comes a sailboat**

sailing by.

**There is a motorboat**

**speeding through waves.**

A fireboat rushes

# to put out a fire.

**A ferryboat carries**

**people and cars.**

# There goes a fishing boat

out to sea.

# Here comes a cruise ship

**into the harbor.**

# Here comes a tugboat

# to help the ship dock.

# Here is the tugboat

**pushing and pulling.**

Here is the ship

at the dock.

Here are the workers

loading the ship.

Here are the people

going on board.

Here are the people

waving good-bye.

There goes the ship

sailing away.

*Bon voyage.*